MR. MEN
AND
little Miss

ANNUAL 1998

"I'm Mr Nosey. I love being nosey – do you?" See if you can find me on every page.

Illustrations: Adam and Giles Hargreaves
Original text: Roger Hargreaves   New text: John Malam
Cover design: Paul Dronsfield   Design: Maggie Aldred

MR. MEN and LITTLE MISS™ & ©
1997 Mrs. Hargreaves. Printed and published under licence from Price Stern Sloan Inc., Los Angeles. All rights reserved. Published in Great Britain by World International Ltd., Deanway Technology Centre, Wilmslow Road, Handforth, Cheshire SK9 3FB. Printed in Italy.
ISBN 0 7498 3381 5

£5.50
UK only

MR. MEN AND *little Miss*

Annual 1998

"I'm Little Miss Curious. Are you as curious as I am? I wonder what could be inside my Mr Men and Little Miss Annual? If I read these two pages, then I'll soon find out where all my favourite friends are – and then I can turn to their pages straightaway!"

Contents

THIS WAY !

Mr Tickle

1 Mr Tickle has the longest, bendiest arms you will ever see. Now, if you think those arms get in Mr Tickle's way, you are in for a very big surprise.

2 Mr Tickle uses his stretchy, twisty arms to do things that you or I can only dream of. Mr Tickle's arms are very useful arms indeed, as you will see.

3 On Monday, Mr Tickle went to Buttercup Cottage. This was Little Miss Scatterbrain's house. She was outside, looking through a window.

4 She was outside because she had locked herself out of her own house. So, Mr Tickle reached in through the window – and opened her front door!

5 On Tuesday, the wind blew Mr Chatterbox's hat on to the roof of Chatterbox Cottage. For once, Mr Chatterbox didn't know what to say.

6 It was the easiest thing in the world for Mr Tickle to stretch up and reach the hat – then Mr Chatterbox started talking and didn't stop!

7 On Wednesday, Mr Tickle went to Horseshoe Cottage to see Little Miss Lucky. They were going to a party. He rang the bell. There was no reply.

8 He put one arm through the letterbox. It went up the stairs into Little Miss Lucky's bedroom. She was asleep – until he tapped her on the shoulder!

9 On Thursday, Mr Tickle bumped into his old friend Mr Forgetful. Well, actually, Mr Forgetful tripped over one of Mr Tickle's long arms.

10 Mr Forgetful fell flat on his face. He didn't look very happy, so Mr Tickle cheered him up the only way he knew how – by tickling him all over!

11 On Friday, Mr Tickle saw Mr Nosey peeping from behind a balloon. When he reached out and popped it, Mr Nosey fell on his nose!

12 On Saturday and Sunday, Mr Tickle stayed at home. He cleaned his windows and swept his carpets – without getting out of bed!

Mr Snow's snowstorm

"I'm Mr Snow. I'm going to show you how you can make a snowstorm in a jar. Then I'm going to tell you about snowflakes. If anyone knows all about snowflakes, it's me!"

You will need...

- a jar with a screw top
- a spoonful of dessicated coconut (or silver glitter)
- a Christmas card
- water
- plasticine
- sticky tape
- me! (a cake decoration of a snowman)

1 Unscrew the lid from the jar. Press a large piece of plasticine into the inside of the lid.

2 Press the snowman firmly into the plasticine

3 Cut out a snowy picture from a Christmas card. Tape the picture to the outside of the jar. The top of the picture should point towards the bottom of the jar. The picture should wrap only about halfway round the jar.

4 Fill the jar with water. Add the dessicated coconut (or glitter).

5 Screw the lid tightly onto the jar. Turn the jar upside down. Shake it and watch as the snow falls around Mr Snow.

Snowflakes

- Snowflakes have six sides.

- Snowflakes are made from frozen water.

- No two snowflakes are the same – they all have different six-sided shapes.

- Millions of snowflakes fall in a single snowstorm.

Whose house is this?

This is Weekend Cottage. Do you know who lives here? You'll soon find out whose house it is when you follow the five paths. Only one of them will take you to the front door of Weekend Cottage.

Orange cream sweets

You will need...

- 400 grams of icing sugar
- 1/2 teaspoon of lemon juice
- 1 orange

"I'm Little Miss Greedy. Would you like to make orange cream sweets with me? They're my yummy favourites! Ask a grown up to help you."

1 Put the icing sugar into a large bowl.

2 Grate the orange rind on to the icing sugar.

3 Add the lemon juice. Squeeze a little orange juice on to the icing sugar too.

4 With your hands, work the mixture into a firm, smooth mass. If it won't keep together, add more juice until it does.

5 When the mixture is just firm enough, turn it on to a pastry board. Dust a rolling pin with icing sugar. Roll the mixture out until it is about 5mm thick.

6 Cut your orange creams into small rounds. Leave them to dry and harden on greaseproof paper. When they are dry on both sides, they're ready to eat – I can't wait!

11

Little Miss Bossy

1 This is the story of what happened to little Miss Bossy the day she lost her voice. This was the day she tried to be bossy, but wasn't.

2 To begin with, she didn't know she had lost her voice. Everything seemed just the same when she woke up. As usual, the birds were singing.

3 And as usual, she opened her bedroom window and shouted at them to be quiet. Or did she? Well, she tried to shout, but nothing happened.

4 Little Miss Bossy looked puzzled. The birds looked puzzled, too. Then they carried on singing, louder than ever. This was not a usual day at all!

6 And do you know what she saw? It was not a pretty sight. Little Miss Bossy had got the sorest throat you could ever think of. UGH!

5 Little Miss Bossy went into her bathroom. She stood in front of the mirror. She opened her mouth as wide as she could, and looked inside.

7 You see, the day before she had had one of her bossiest days ever. All day long she had bossed people around. She had told Mr Lazy to wake up.

8 She had tried to talk to Little Miss Chatterbox. But the only way she could make herself heard was by shouting at the top of her voice.

9 Then she had seen Mr Messy painting a picture. He was making a terrible mess, of course. So Little Miss Bossy just had to tell him to clean it all up.

10 She went to Earlybird Cottage to see Little Miss Late. But she wasn't ready, and so Little Miss Bossy ordered her around until she was.

11 Well, after a bossy day like that, it was not surprising that Little Miss Bossy had lost her voice. There was only one thing for her to do.

12 She went back to bed. Perhaps her voice would come back tomorrow. Then she could have a bossy day, as usual. What do you think?

"Today's the day at last!" said Mr Greedy. "Today's the day me and my gigantic, roly-poly tummy are going to Mr Mischief's house for tea. I do hope there will be lots of sticky strawberry jam sandwiches, wibbly-wobbly jellies and gooey chocolate cakes. I'm feeling hungrier than ever!"

But Mr Greedy was in for a big surprise. He should have known that Mr Mischief liked to play tricks.

It was a very long way to Mr Mischief's house. Mr Greedy began to think that Mr Mischief might start without him, and eat all the food!

There would be no sticky strawberry jam sandwiches,

no wibbly-wobbly jellies and absolutely no gooey chocolate cakes!

Mr Greedy held on to his tummy and started to run.

But he needn't have worried. Mr Mischief hadn't eaten the food. In fact, he hadn't even touched it.

So, when Mr Greedy saw the table piled high with, you've guessed it, sticky strawberry jam sandwiches, wibbly-wobbly jellies and gooey chocolate cakes, his tummy seemed to grow bigger.

"Can we start now?" asked Mr Greedy, greedily.

Mr Mischief said he wanted Mr Greedy to play a guessing game. He said he wanted Mr Greedy to close his

guessing game

eyes, and try to guess what he was eating.

Mr Greedy should have known that Mr Mischief was about to play a trick on him. But all he could think of was the tasty food.

"Close your eyes and open your mouth," said Mr Mischief.

Mr Greedy was expecting Mr Mischief to pop a strawberry jam sandwich into his mouth.

"Uggh!" said Mr Greedy. "That tastes like soggy cornflakes!"

"Let's try something else," said Mr Mischief, trying not to laugh.

Mr Greedy was hoping for a mouthful of jelly. But instead …

"Yuk! That tastes like cold porridge!" he spluttered.

"One more," said Mr Mischief.

"I hope it's chocolate cake," began Mr Greedy, who then looked startled and said, "Arrgh! It tastes like burnt toast!"

Well, that was enough for Mr Greedy. He opened his eyes and said to Mr Mischief: "You've played a trick on me!"

"But have I?" said Mr Mischief. "You know so much about food, that I couldn't catch you out. You guessed the right answer each time! That means there's only one thing left to do … and you know what that is, don't you?"

"Yes I do!" said Mr Greedy, rubbing his tummy. "Now it really is time to eat the food!"

Which is what he did, as fast as he could, just in case Mr Mischief played another trick on him!

Spot the difference

"I'm Little Miss Scatterbrain, and I live in Buttercup Cottage. Well, I think I do. You see, I keep on forgetting where I live. Here are two pictures of me and my house. Look at them closely. Can you spot five things that are different in the bottom picture? When you think you've found the differences, turn to page 61 to see if you are right."

Count with me

"I'm Little Miss Wise. Can you help me?
I'm counting out red, green and blue beads.
I'm going to make them into necklaces.
I'm putting them in groups of five.
Would you draw more beads for me,
so that each group has five? Thank you."

Wordsquare puzzle

"I'm Mr Muddle. I always get things mixed up. On the other page is a square full of muddled letters. Can you find ten words hidden in it? Look forwards and backwards, up and down. Draw lines through them when you find each word. I've done one to start you off. When you've found them, go to page 61 to see if you are right."

Tick them off as you find the hidden words:

☐ ball   ☐ apple   ☐ banana

☐ book   ☐ bread   ☐ buttons

☐ **radio**

☐ **biscuit**

a	l	l	e	r	b	m	u
s	b	r	e	a	d	f	x
n	o	a	z	j	r	e	t
o	o	d	n	u	b	l	o
t	k	i	q	a	k	p	p
t	j	o	l	v	n	p	a
u	c	l	z	m	l	a	e
b	b	i	s	c	u	i	t

☐ **teapot**

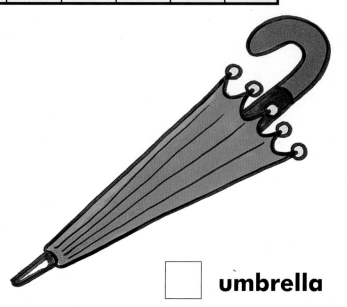

☐ **umbrella**

The missing

[Little Miss Neat] lived in Twopin Cottage. It was called Twopin Cottage because it was as neat as **2** new [nails]. Even the pretty [flowers] in her [garden] were nice and neat. There was nothing out of place. Last week, [Little Miss Neat] had a party for **3** of her friends. It was a party with lots of [cakes] to eat. It was a party with [balloons], and it was a party with games to play. Little Miss Magic, Little Miss Giggles and [Little Miss Tidy] were at the party. First they played pass the [parcel]. Then they played musical [chairs]. They did a [jigsaw] puzzle after their tea. It was a picture of a [horse]. There were supposed to be **100** pieces in the jigsaw. But they could only find **99**. One piece was missing! [Little Miss Giggles] thought that was very funny. [Little Miss Neat] didn't think it was funny at all. "We must look everywhere!" she

jigsaw piece

said. They looked behind the , under the

and inside the tin! But the missing piece was

nowhere to be found. "I think I know where it might be,"

said . "It might have been tidied away in another ."

They looked in the other boxes. But it wasn't there.

They looked in an box. They looked in a box.

They looked in a box too! But it wasn't in any of

them. "Let me try some magic," said . "Open!" she

said to the . It wasn't there. "Lift!" she said

to the . It wasn't there either. Then picked

up a stripey . It was 's bag. Inside was the

missing piece! "You had it all the time!" she said. "Now

we can finish the puzzle!"

21

Mr Nosey

1 It was the first day of spring. It was a good day for tidying up, when everyone helped each other to clean their houses. Mr Nosey held a big brush.

2 Off he went to the messiest house he knew. He had decided to help Mr Messy tidy his house. But really, he wanted to look inside, just to be nosey.

3 The first thing Mr Nosey did at Mr Messy's house was peep through the keyhole. He couldn't see anything. A messy cobweb was in the way!

4 Mr Nosey used his brush to brush the dusty old cobweb away. Then he peeped through Mr Messy's keyhole again. "That's better," he said.

5 Mr Nosey could see lots of boxes, lots of drawers, lots of books, and lots of interesting things he wanted to poke his nosey nose into.

6 Mr Nosey opened the door and went inside. Mr Messy was nowhere to be seen. "I'm sure he won't mind if I look around," said Mr Nosey.

7 First, he picked up a big box. He shook it. Something rattled inside. "Mmm, this sounds fun," said Mr Nosey. "I wonder what it could be?"

8 Mr Nosey got the surprise of his life. He almost jumped right out of his skin when he lifted the lid off the box ... and up popped a jack-in-the-box!

9 He ran into the kitchen. But slipped on a half-eaten banana and knocked over a great big pile of cups and saucers, pots and pans. CRASH!

10 He looked in the bedroom. "I wonder what these books are?" he said. But as he took one off the bookcase, they all came tumbling down!

11 And that was when Mr Messy came along to find out what all the noise was. "Er ... hello," said Mr Nosey. "I've come to tidy your house."

12 "But I like it messy," said Mr Messy. "I can see you've made it messier than ever!" Mr Nosey thought that was funny, and began to laugh.

23

Can you remember?

"I'm Mr Perfect. Can you remember as much as I can? You'll soon find out how much you can remember when you try this memory game. All you have to do is look at the things drawn on these two pages. Then close the book.
How many things can you remember?"

24

Little Miss Busy and

L ittle Miss Busy is always as busy as a bee. She isn't happy unless she is busy. For instance, when Mr Sneeze runs out of tissues, she makes herself as busy as she can by dashing off to his house to fetch not one, but one hundred and one tissues! When she sees Little Miss Tidy all on her own tidying up after a messy party, she makes herself so busy that in no time at all everything is neat and tidy again.

One day, Little Miss Busy went for a walk in the park. She felt like being busy, but she couldn't decide what to do.

Just then she saw a horseshoe lying on the grass. It gave her an idea. "Well," she said, out loud, "I know that horseshoes are supposed to be lucky. Who can I give this lucky horseshoe to, so they can have lots of good luck?"

Little Miss Busy picked up the horseshoe and said, "Little Miss Brainy could do with some good luck today!" So, feeling busy, off she went to see her clever friend.

Today was a special day for

Who has spilled yellow paint?

the lucky horseshoe

Little Miss Brainy. To show just how brainy she was, she was answering lots of different questions all day long. The trouble was, she wasn't very good

at it. For instance, when Little Miss Greedy asked her to guess how many jam doughnuts she had eaten for breakfast, Little Miss Brainy didn't know the answer. When Little Miss Magic asked her how many letter a's there were in 'abracadabra', Little Miss Brainy counted the letter b's instead. And, when Little Miss Somersault asked her what the difference was between a handstand and a hatstand, Little Miss Brainy got all muddled up

and said, "You hang hats on a handstand!"

Just at that moment Little Miss Busy arrived with the lucky horseshoe. "I've brought you a lovely surprise," she said to Little Miss Brainy. "This lucky horseshoe will bring you lots of good luck. Now you'll get all the answers right!"

Little Miss Brainy took the horseshoe. She held it tightly in both hands. Then she started to smile. "Does anyone have another question for me?" she asked.

Join the paint spots together to find out who it is.

"Yes, I do," said Little Miss Greedy, again. "How many eggs did I have for breakfast?"

Little Miss Brainy thought hard. "Mmm," she said, "I think I know the answer. You ate seventeen boiled eggs. Am I right?"

Little Miss Greedy could scarcely believe her ears. "That's absolutely right!" she said, in complete amazement.

Then it was Little Miss Magic's turn. "What can you hold without touching it?" she said.

Little Miss Brainy looked

puzzled. She held the lucky horseshoe more tightly than before and said, "Your breath! Am I right?"

Little Miss Magic could hardly believe that Little Miss Brainy had given the correct answer to such a tricky question.

Last of all, Little Miss Somersault asked her what the difference was between a cartwheel and a carthorse.

"That's a funny question," said Little Miss Brainy. She began to think. "Mmm," she said.

But before she could answer,

Little Miss Busy called out, "Look! A horse! It's lost one of its shoes. In fact, I think it's lost this horseshoe," she said, pointing to the lucky horseshoe.

Little Miss Busy felt like being busy again, so she took the horseshoe to the horse, who was very pleased to have it back.

"I'm still waiting for an answer to my question," said Little Miss Somersault. But without the lucky horseshoe, Little Miss Brainy didn't know the answer.

"Mmm," Little Miss Brainy said again. Then, quick as a flash, she ran after the horse as it galloped away. "Excuse me," she called out. "Can I borrow one of your horseshoes, please? I need some more

good luck straightaway!"

That was the last anyone saw of Little Miss Brainy that day.

"Well," said Little Miss Busy. "Fancy that. What a busy day it's been after all. I've helped Little Miss Brainy and a horse today. How busy I've been!"

Boat sandwiches

You will need...

- 2 long bread rolls
- butter or margarine
- cheese spread in a tube
- 4 slices of ham
- 4 slices of cucumber
- 4 cocktail sticks

"I'm Mr Funny. Look at my funny-looking sandwiches – I think they look just like little boats. Ask a grown-up to help you make some."

1 Cut each roll in half lengthways. Spread the halves with butter or margarine.

2 Squeeze a wiggly line of cheese spread along the bread.

3 Put a piece of rolled-up ham onto the cheese spread.

4 To make a sail for each boat, push a cocktail stick through a slice of cucumber. Then push it through the ham and onto the bread.

Colour with me

"I'm Little Miss Naughty. I want to do some colouring, but all my paint has dripped out of my tin. Have you followed the yellow paint spots across the pages? I don't have any paint left. Can you help? Use your own colours to finish this picture for me. Thank you!"

Nonsense Land

Dot-to-dot with Little Miss Fickle

"I'm Little Miss Fickle. I live in Dandelion Cottage. When you join the dots together you'll soon find out what my lovely house looks like."

I'm Little Miss Neat. I live next door to Little Miss Fickle, in Twopin Cottage. Read about me on page 20!

Picture crossword

"I'm Little Miss Giggles. I live in Chuckle Cottage. Would you help me to finish this picture crossword puzzle? I've done the first letters of each word. When you do the rest, you'll know where five of my friends live. Then turn to page 61 to see if you are right."

1 across
Little Miss Lucky
lives in  Cottage

1 down
Little Miss Scatterbrain
lives in Cottage

2 down
Little Miss Fickle
lives in Cottage

3 down
Little Miss Neat
lives in Cottage

4 down
Little Miss Shy
lives in Cottage

¹B
²D
³T
⁴T
¹H

Around the

"I'm Mr Tall. I go all over the world looking at tall buildings and towers. Here are some photographs I have taken on my travels."

America
Empire State Building in New York City
Look how small it makes the other buildings look!
448 metres (1,472 feet) high

America
World Trade Center in New York City
This tall building is actually two towers, side by side.
411 metres (1,350 feet) high

Egypt
Pyramid of Khufu near Cairo
In front of the pyramid is a statue called the Sphinx.
146 metres (480 feet) high

world with Mr Tall

Next time I go round the world, I'm going to Kuala Lumpur, Malaysia. There I'll see the Petronas Towers, which will soon be the tallest building in the whole world. It will be 452 metres (1,483 feet) high!

Great Britain
Canary Wharf in London
This is the tallest building in the whole of the country.
244 metres (800 feet) high

France
Eiffel Tower in Paris
A road runs between the giant legs of this famous tower.
300 metres (984 feet) high

Canada
CN Tower in Toronto
This is the world's tallest freestanding structure.
553 metres (1,815 feet) high

Make music

"I'm Mr Noisy. I like making music. The noisier the better! You can make your own music too, by copying what I do."

Mr Noisy's ringing glass

After a bit of practice I can make the glass ring! Can you?

1 First I hold a wine glass flat on a table by its base.

2 Then I rub a finger moistened with water round and round the top of the glass. It works best if I press down quite firmly.

Mr Noisy's yoghurt pot shaker

My yoghurt pot shaker makes a great sound! Does yours?

1 First I put a few dried peas or lentils into a clean, dry yoghurt pot.

2 Then I fasten a paper lid over the pot with an elastic band.

with Mr Noisy

1 First I cut two oblongs from the side of a plastic yoghurt pot.

2 I put the oblongs together so that they both curve outwards.

3 Then I stick the oblongs together at one end only with sticky tape. This is called a reed.

4 I twist a piece of paper into a cone. Sticky tape holds it together for me.

5 I cut the pointed end of the cone off.

6 Then I push the reed into the hole in the end of the cone. The taped end goes in first. The untaped end sticks out. Sticky tape holds the reed to the cone.

To get the best sound I pinch my lips together a bit to make them thin. Then I blow through my reed.

Mr Dizzy is lost!

Mr Dizzy's house is on the side of a very steep hill. He's been shopping and can't find his way back up the hill. Can you show him the way home?

Little Miss Trouble

1 Little Miss Trouble is one of those people who makes trouble wherever she goes. But she doesn't always get her own way, as you'll see.

2 One day she ate Little Miss Greedy's cake. She said that Little Miss Bossy had eaten it. Now that caused a lot of trouble, as you can imagine.

3 Little Miss Greedy shouted at Little Miss Bossy. Little Miss Bossy shouted back, of course. And then they both shouted at Little Miss Trouble!

4 Then she told Mr Rush that Mr Lazy had a surprise for him. Mr Rush ran to Mr Lazy's house and knocked on his door as hard as he could.

6 Then Little Miss Trouble told Little Miss Helpful about a cat who was stuck at the top of a tree. Little Miss Helpful climbed up to help the cat.

5 Mr Lazy didn't like being woken up. He squirted water out of his window, all over Mr Rush. "That's not a very nice surprise!" said Mr Rush.

7 But there wasn't really a cat in the tree at all. "Help!" she called. "I can't get down!" It was Little Miss Somersault who helped her out of the tree.

8 But then, Little Miss Trouble tried to play a trick on Mr Mischief. And just for once it was Little Miss Trouble who got the surprise.

9 She told Mr Mischief that Mr Chatterbox wanted to talk to him on the telephone. Mr Mischief listened, but there was no one there.

10 "Actually," said Mr Mischief, pretending that he could hear someone, "Mr Chatterbox wants to talk to you."

12 Little Miss Trouble jumped up, banged her head and then dropped the phone on her toe! OUCH! She caused no more trouble that day!

11 Little Miss Trouble put the phone to her ear. Mr Mischief ran off and picked up the other phone. "BOO!" he shouted, loudly.

Mr Daydream's

First I dreamt I was in **Europe** skiing in the Alps. But I fell over and rolled down like a giant snowball, and I ended up in …

… **Africa**. I was in the jungle, riding on the back of a big grey elephant. But when a crocodile snapped at me I was whisked away to …

… **North America**, where I was dressed as a cowboy! But just as I was about to climb onto a horse, my dream changed and I found I was in …

… **South America!** I was in the rainforest. There were birds everywhere. But as I was about to take a photograph of some colourful parrots in the trees, my dream moved me on to …

best dream ever

"I'm Mr Daydream. I love to daydream about going to faraway countries. In my best daydream ever I visited every continent on the Earth – all seven of them. Let me tell you what happened."

... **Asia**, where it was hot and sunny. I was feeling hungry, and went to a restaurant for something to eat. But I wasn't very good at eating with chopsticks, so on I went to ...

... **Antarctica!** I was at the South Pole. Brrr! It was freezing. Even the penguins thought it was cold. But luckily for me I didn't stay long, and soon I was in ...

... I woke up and realised I'd been daydreaming again!

... **Australasia**, where I tried to throw a boomerang. But oh dear! It came back and clonked me on the head, and that was when ...

Mr Happy and

It was a very windy day. It was so windy that leaves were blowing off the trees, and people's umbrellas were being blown inside out.

When Mr Happy went into his garden, something black and shiny blew right past him.

"That looks like Mr Uppity's top hat!" he called out. "Will someone help me catch it?"

But no one heard him. The wind was blowing so hard that it blew the words right out of his mouth, blew them high up into the air, over his house and far, far away until they were no more than a tiny little whisper.

Mr Happy ran after Mr Uppity's top hat all on his own.

He ran as fast as he could. He ran so fast that he was soon out of breath, and his smile started to turn down at the corners.

But then, just when he was about to give up, an extra big gust of wind blew him right off his feet. Up, up and up he went. Over the houses. Over the trees. Then down again. And there, lying just in front of him was Mr Uppity's shiny black top hat.

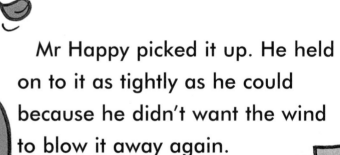

Mr Happy picked it up. He held on to it as tightly as he could because he didn't want the wind to blow it away again.

the windy day

Mr Happy went straight to Mr Uppity's house and rang his doorbell. RING! RING!

He waited. No reply. He rang the bell again, three times. RING! RING! RINGGG!

Very slowly the front door opened. It only opened a little way, just far enough for Mr Happy to see Mr Uppity peeping at him.

"What do you want?" snapped Mr Uppity, rather rudely.

Mr Happy held the top hat in front of him. Before he could say a single word, Mr Uppity flung the door wide open and snatched the hat!

"I thought I had lost my hat for good," said Mr Uppity. "Where did you find it?"

Mr Happy told him what had happened.

"Well, I'm jolly glad you did find my hat," said Mr Uppity. "I can't go anywhere without it. I've been miserable all day long – but now you've cheered me up!"

And with that, Mr Uppity put his hat on his head, held his chin up high and walked off along his garden path.

"Mind the wind doesn't blow it off again," called out Mr Happy.

But it was too late. The wind crept up quickly behind Mr Uppity, and blew his hat straight up into the air.

Mr Happy watched as Mr Uppity chased after it. "Oh dear," he said, in a little voice. "I think it's time I was somewhere else."

Mr Happy decided to go home. He'd had quite enough running about for one day. But when he arrived, there was a surprise waiting for him.

Caught in a tree in his garden was a balloon.

"Oh dear," said Mr Happy. "A lost balloon."

Mr Happy climbed the tree. He reached out to the balloon, grabbed hold of the string and ... the strongest gust of wind he had felt all day blew and blew and blew.

It blew Mr Happy and the balloon out of the tree. He held on to the balloon string as tightly as he could.

Up, up and up he went. Over the houses. Over the trees. Then down again ...

... He landed right back where he had started, at Mr Uppity's house!

Unfortunately he landed in a prickly bush. POP! went the balloon. "OUCH!" said Mr Happy.

Mr Uppity came out to see what was going on. He seemed very pleased about something.

"Look," said Mr Uppity, pointing to his head. "I got my top hat back!"

Sure enough, there, without a shadow of a doubt, was Mr Uppity's shiny black top hat, perched carefully on top of his head, right where it belonged.

Just to make certain that the wind didn't blow it off again, Mr Happy tied one end of the balloon string to Mr Uppity's top hat. He gave him the other end to hold on to.

"You won't lose your hat again now," said Mr Happy.

And he was right. The next time the wind blew, up went Mr Uppity's hat – but he pulled on the string and it came straight back down again!

Mr Bump

1 Mr Bump can't help bumping into things. Even when he's fast asleep he dreams about walking into trees and bumping his head. OUCH!

2 But then he wakes up with such a surprise that he immediately rolls over, falls out of bed and bumps onto the floor! OUCH! again.

3 One night, after he fell out of bed, he couldn't get back to sleep. So he looked out of his window, just to see what his garden looked like at night.

4 He saw a funny light in his garden. It was Mr Nosey shining a torch. Mr Bump opened the window, and just as he was about to call out …

5 … out he fell. He landed in a bush. On his head. Upside-down. And everywhere was very, very dark. He couldn't see where he was at all.

6 Along came Mr Nosey. He shone his torch into the bush. "What's going on?" he said, talking to the bush. "Get me out!" said Mr Bump.

7 Poor old Mr Nosey. He got such a fright. He thought the bush had spoken to him! He didn't know that it was Mr Bump. Mr Nosey ran away.

8 Mr Bump tried to climb out of the bush. But he slipped and bumped onto the ground. CRASH! "It's dark," he said. "I can't see where I'm going."

9 He stood up … and bumped his head on the branch of a tree. OUCH! "Everywhere looks so different at night," he said. "I must be careful."

10 Instead of walking, he began to crawl on his hands and knees … straight into a puddle of water. SPLASH! Mr Bump was soaked to the skin.

12 He picked up the round, hard thing. It was Mr Nosey's torch. "Now I can see in the dark," he said. And off he went, straight back to his bed.

11 Up he got, as fast as he could. But, oh dear! He tripped on something round and hard, and over he went. BUMP! on his head. OUCH!

A day at

and were at the . The was shining and the were making a lot of noise. "Would you like an ?" asked . "I can stretch an over to the without having to move from my ." reached out past a , past a , and then past a long thing poking out from under a big . "I know what that is," said

"Come out ," he said. But didn't move. He was lying on his , fast asleep. And he was snoring! decided to have some fun. He found a seagull's in the sand. He reached out with his long

mr. Tickle

the seaside

and he tickled Mr Nosey's  with the feather. That

stopped him snoring! Then Mr Nosey chased Mr Tickle past

the ice cream van and all over the  Then, oh dear!

Mr Bump bumped into them both! Mr Nosey's nose went

and Mr Tickle's fell into the  had

to stretch out an extra-long bendy to fetch it back.

"Sorry," said Mr Bump.  rubbed his .

"This will make it better," said Mr Tickle, and he stuck a  on

the end of Mr Nosey's nose! Afterwards they made

for Mr Bump to bump into. Then it was time to say "bye bye" to

the until another day.

Copy colour with Little Miss Splendid

Little Miss Splendid looks absolutely fabulous in her splendid spotty hat and high-heeled shoes. Make your picture look just as splendid.

52

Copy colour with Mr Funny

Mr Funny lives in a house that looks like a teapot, and he drives a car that looks like a shoe. Make your picture look just as funny.

Fizzy lemonade

You will need...

- 3 lemons
- 175g of sugar
- 900ml (1.5 pints) of boiling water
- 1 teaspoon of bicarbonate of soda

"I'm Little Miss Star. I'm having a party. I've made orange cream sweets, boat sandwiches and now I'm making fizzy lemonade. Ask a grown-up to help you."

1 Wash the lemons. Grate a thin layer of the lemon rind off. Make sure you grate all over the lemons. Mind your fingers!

2 Put the grated lemon rind and sugar into a large basin or jug.

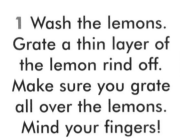

3 Ask a grown-up to pour the boiling water into the jug. Stir the mixture. Leave to cool for a few minutes. Stir occasionally.

4 Cut the lemons in half. Squeeze the juice out and add it to the mixture.

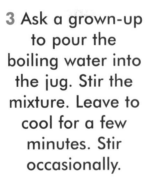

5 Strain the lemonade to remove any bits.

6 To make the lemonade fizzy, add the bicarbonate of soda. Stir well. Serve chilled. Enjoy it!

Chuckle with Little Miss Giggles

Little Miss Curious, why did the owl make me laugh?

I don't know. Tell me.

Because he was a hoot!

Mr Jelly, what wobbles when it flies?

I don't know. Tell me.

A jellycopter!

Little Miss Brainy, what's hairy and coughs?

I don't know. Tell me.

A coconut with a cold!

Little Miss Dotty, do you know why you eat biscuits?

I don't know. Tell me.

Because you're crackers!

Fast, faster, fastest

"I'm Mr Rush. I go everywhere as fast as I can – and so do these five machines. But do you know how fast they go? Decide what order they go in, from the fastest to the slowest. Then turn to page 61 to see if you are right."

Sports car

Bicycle

56

with Mr Rush

Space Shuttle rocket

Aeroplane

Double decker bus

Did you know that a person only walks at about four miles per hour? That wouldn't do for me!

Mr Clumsy's

Mr Clumsy had gone to watch a football match. As you probably know, Mr Clumsy is very, very clumsy. If something can go wrong, then Mr Clumsy makes sure that it does. However, the good thing about Mr Clumsy is that he doesn't seem to mind. He just smiles and carries on.

Well, there he was, minding his own business, watching the football match ... when Mr Bump bumped into the goalpost. Now Mr Bump's team needed someone to take his place. And guess who they picked.

BANG!

Well, as you can imagine, Mr Clumsy isn't really the best person to be picked to play football.

The first thing he did was run onto the pitch and kick the ball so hard that it burst. BANG!

Luckily for Mr Clumsy there was another football, but for some reason no one wanted to kick it to him.

"You go and be goalkeeper," said Mr Tickle.

Mr Clumsy soon got fed up being all on his own in the goal. He started to jump up and down, just to see if he could touch the top of the goalpost.

Then he decided to swing from the goalpost. That was a big mistake. The goalpost creaked then snapped in half. Mr Clumsy tumbled to the ground. And soon he was all knotted up inside the net!

game of football

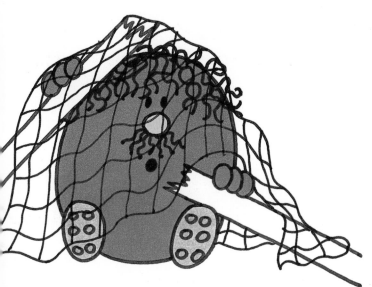

After Mr Strong had mended the goal, Mr Bump came back on to finish playing the rest of the game.

"I think I'll go and sit down," said Mr Clumsy.

"Why don't you be our cheerleader?" said Mr Tickle. "Then you can jump up and down as much as you like."

And that was exactly what Mr Clumsy did. He jumped up and down, did cartwheels, clapped his hands and sang songs.

All went well until he got fed up again. When he pressed a button on an electric lawnmower, off it went, zig-zagging all over the football pitch with him holding on to it.

And that was the end of the football match. Everyone ran off, leaving Mr Clumsy to cut the grass in his own clumsy way.

Join the MR.MEN & little Miss CLUB

If you know a Mr Men and Little Miss fan, here's your chance to give them a very special treat. Imagine their delight when they receive a personal letter from Mr Happy and Little Miss Giggles, a club badge with their name, and a superb Welcome Pack.

The Welcome Pack ✔ Membership card ✔ Personalised badge ✔ Exclusive Club cassette with Mr Men stories and songs ✔ Mr Men keyring ✔ Mr Men sticker book ✔ Tiny Mr Men flock model ✔ Club pencil ✔ Personal Mr Men notebook ✔ Mr Men bendy pen ✔ Mr Men eraser ✔ Mr Men book mark ✔ Birthday card ✔ Christmas card ✔ Copy of Mr Men magazine

Take a look at all of the great things in the Welcome Pack. If it were on sale in the shops, the Pack alone would cost around £12.00. But a year's membership is just £8.99 (plus 73p postage) with a 14 day money-back guarantee if you are not delighted.

To apply simply fill in the coupon below (or a photocopy) and send to Mr Men and Little Miss Club, Happyland, PO Box 142, Horsham RH13 5FJ, or call 01403 242727 for immediate enrolment (credit cards only).

How thrilled they'll be to get a card from the Mr Men and Little Misses on their birthday and again at Christmas. And the whole family will love the regular newsletter crammed with special offers, privileges and news.

Club T-Shirt Save £2

Join today and get the Club T-Shirt for just £3.99, a saving of £2 on the usual price. Choose from ages 3-4, 5-6 and 7-8. Order below

Please note: Exact contents of the Welcome Pack may change from time to time. Allow 28 days for delivery. After 30/6/98 please call to check price. All communications (except the Welcome Pack) will be via parents/guardians. Promoter: Robell Media Promotions Limited, registered in England number 2852153.

MR.MEN and LITTLE MISS™ & © 1997 Mrs. Roger Hargreaves

To be completed by an adult.

Please enrol the following as a member in the Mr Men & Little Miss Club at £9.72 (inc. post and packaging)

Member's Full Name: _____ Member's Address: _____

_____ Post Code: _____ Date of birth: __/__/

Your Name: _____ Address (if different): _____

_____ Post Code: _____

Name of child's parent or guardian (if not you): _____

Please also send me __ Club T-Shirt(s) at £3.99. Tick size(s) ❏ age 3-4   ❏ age 5-6   ❏ age 7-8

❏ I enclose a cheque or postal order for £_____ payable to Mr Men & Little Miss Club

❏ Please charge the sum of £_____ to my Access/Visa account.

Card number: [ ][ ][ ][ ][ ][ ][ ][ ][ ][ ][ ][ ][ ][ ][ ][ ] Expiry Date: ____/____

Robell Club

Data Protection Act: If you do **not** wish to receive other children's offers from us or companies we recommend, please tick this box ❏

Answers

Page 33 – Picture crossword

```
        ¹B
         U
         T
         T                ²D
         E                 A                    ³T
    ⁴T   R                 N                     W
    ¹H O R S E S H O E     D                     I
    I    C                 E                     N
    M    U                 L                     ...
```

(Crossword grid)

Across: HORSESHOE
Down: 1 BUTTERCUP, 2 DANDELION, 3 TWOPIN, 4 THIMBLE

Page 16 – Spot the difference

The five different things are:

1 A curtain is missing

2 A tree trunk is different

3 There is a bird in the tree

4 There is a flower in the bush

5 Little Miss Scatterbrain's left arm is missing

Page 18 – Wordsquare puzzle

a	l	l	e	r	b	m	u
s	b	r	e	a	d	f	x
n	o	a	z	j	r	e	t
o	o	d	n	u	b	l	o
t	k	i	q	a	k	p	p
t	j	o	l	v	n	p	a
u	c	l	z	m	l	a	e
b	b	i	s	c	u	i	t

Page 56 – Fast, faster, fastest with Mr Rush

The machines go in this order:

1 Space shuttle rocket

2 Aeroplane

3 Sports car

4 Double decker bus

5 Bicycle

A maze for Mr Nosey

"I'm Mr Nosey. I like to look inside other people's houses. I stare through windows, peer through letterboxes, and when I close one eye I can even peep through keyholes. Once, I enjoyed being nosey so much that I got lost! It took me a long time to find the way back to my own house. Which way did I go?"

62